Say Hello on the Farm!

Ian Whybrow   Tim Warnes

BackPACKBOOKS

· NEW YORK

Ready, steady, off we go.
Round the farm to say hello.

Who's that nibbling, half asleep?
Say hello to the drowsy sheep.

Hello, Sheep!
Baaa, baaa, baaa!

Here's the sty – not very big –
Say hello to the little pink pig.

Hello, Pig!

Oink, oink, oink!

Who's on the fence beside her pen?
Say hello to the speckly hen.

Look who's hiding under those sticks.
Say hello to the fluffy chicks.

Look in the barn – who's in here now?
Say hello to the friendly cow.

Who's that paddling in the muck?
Say hello to the splashy duck.

Hello, Duck!
Quack, quack, quack!

Who's in the stable? Yes, of course!
Say hello to the hungry horse.

Hello, Horse!

Neigh, neigh, neigh!

What a lot of animals, my, oh my!
Now it's time to say goodbye.

"Are you ready, Ella Rose? Off you go with your Hellos!"
With a Hello and a big whiskery kiss from You-know-who. – I.W.

For Nick, Anna, Fraser and Alex:
"Hello you Lows!" – T.W.

Text copyright © 2005 by Ian Whybrow
Illustrations copyright © 2005 by Tim Warnes
Moral rights asserted.

This 2006 edition published by Backpack Books
by arrangement with Macmillan Publishers Ltd.

2006 Backpack Books

ISBN-13: 978-0-7607-8399-3
ISBN-10: 0-7607-8399-3

Printed and bound in China

1 3 5 7 9 10 8 6 4 2

First published 2005 by Macmillan Children's Books
a division of Macmillan Publishers Ltd.